MY ADVENTURES
WITH

This book was especially written for
Jessica Mahoney
with love from
Nana & Papa

Adapted by Kate Andresen
ISBN 1 875676 26 0

Dora's Friends Around the World

¡Hola! I am Dora.

Today is Friendship Day!

On Friendship Day, there are Friendship Parades all around the world! We all get together with our friends and celebrate!

And we wear special glowing Friendship Bracelets too!

Oh, no! Swiper swiped the Friendship Bracelets! Now we have to return them to our friends around the world.

"Jessica, will you help us return the Friendship Bracelets?" asked Dora.

"Of course," replied Jessica. "Can Marlie, Kathleen and Charlie come too?"

"Of course!" said Dora as she handed Friendship Bracelets to Jessica, Marlie, Kathleen and Charlie.

"I want to help save Friendship Day too!" Swiper said.

"We'll all go together!" Dora said.

"But where do we go first?" asked Jessica.

"Who do we ask for help when we don't know which way to go?" Dora asked.

"Map! Map!" Dora called out. Map jumped right out of Backpack's side pocket.

"I'm the Map!" he smiled.

"Hola, Map," said Dora. "We need to return these Friendship Bracelets to our friends around the world."

"I know how to return all the Friendship Bracelets! First, you go to the Eiffel Tower in France," said Map.

Map continued, "Then to Mt. Kilimanjaro, the tallest mountain in Tanzania, Africa. Then we need to go to the Winter Palace in Russia, and then across Asia to the Great Wall of China."

"France, Tanzania, Russia, then China," repeated Jessica.

They were ready to start their adventure.

"Let's go, everybody," Dora called out to her friends.

Soon they found themselves in Paris, France. They needed to find the Eiffel Tower.

"Map says we have to follow the road painted with yellow diamonds to get to the Eiffel Tower," said Dora.

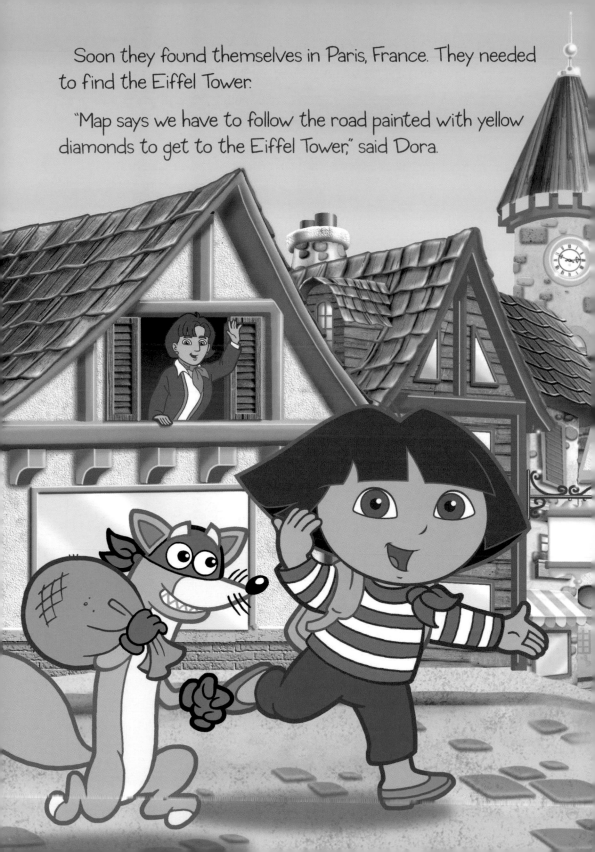

Jessica, Marlie, Kathleen and Charlie ran ahead looking for a road painted with yellow diamonds. They saw circles and squares and then, finally, the bright yellow diamonds.

"This way!" Jessica called to the others. "I can see the Eiffel Tower!"

When they reached the Eiffel Tower, Swiper started returning the Friendship Bracelets he had swiped.

Suddenly, Dora saw Fifi, the skunk. She was trying to swipe the bracelets!

"Oh no! Everybody say, Fifi, no swiping!" called Dora.

Everyone said "Fifi, no swiping" and Fifi scrambled back up the Eiffel Tower.

"That was close," said Jessica. They finished handing out the bracelets and said goodbye to their friends in Paris.

"Dora! Swiper! Marlie! Kathleen! Charlie!" Jessica said. "Where do we go next?"

"What did Map say?" asked Dora.

"France, Tanzania, Russia, China," they called out together. "So next we go to Tanzania in Africa."

They quickly raced over to Tanzania in Africa! They hopped on some elephants to take them through the tall grass.

"The elephants are giving us a ride to the mountain!" exclaimed Dora excitedly.

"Oh look!" called Dora. "I can see a zebra and a lion in the distance!"

"Uh oh! Who is that hiding behind the bushes?" asked Jessica.

It was Sami the hyena.

"He'll try to swipe the Friendship Bracelets!" replied Dora. "Jessica! Marlie! Kathleen! Charlie! Say, no swiping!"

Sami the hyena crept off into the bushes. The Friendship Bracelets were safe!

Soon they came to the foot of
Mt. Kilimanjaro, and their friends were there
to greet them. Dora, Swiper and their friends
handed out the Friendship Bracelets.

When it was time to leave, Jessica asked, "Where do we go next? Russia, yeah! But how will we get to Russia?"

Just then a hot-air balloon landed softly nearby.

"Wow!" exclaimed Jessica.

They said goodbye to their friends in Tanzania and climbed into the hot-air balloon.

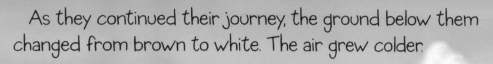

As they continued their journey, the ground below them changed from brown to white. The air grew colder.

They landed by a frozen lake. They shivered with cold.

"Hmm," thought Dora. "We need something to help us get warm. Who always carries everything I need?"

"Backpack!" Jessica answered.

Backpack sprang into action! Out came coats, mittens, hats, and skis for them all. Dora, Jessica, Marlie, Kathleen and Charlie each put on the winter clothes.

Then they continued across the deep, white snow towards the Winter Palace.

Their friends in Russia ran to meet them and get their Friendship Bracelets back.

They didn't see Fomkah the bear, hiding behind a snowman.

Dora turned around and noticed that one snowman looked different from the other. Then she saw Fomkah!

"No swiping!" yelled Dora. Fomkah disappeared into the snow-covered trees.

"That was close," said Dora as she handed out the Friendship Bracelets to her Russian friends.

The bag of bracelets was getting lighter, but there was still one more stop.

When they arrived in China, their friends were also celebrating Friendship Day. Colourful lanterns lit up the Great Wall and everybody was flying beautiful kites.

Dora, Jessica, Marlie, Kathleen and Charlie gave out the Friendship Bracelets.

Just then, Ying-Ying the weasel came riding along on his bike.
He was heading for Swiper, and the bag of bracelets.

"Oh no. No swiping!" everyone called out loudly.

Soon they had finished handing out the bracelets to their friends in China and it was time to go home.

"What an adventure!" said Jessica. "We've visited France, Tanzania, Russia, and China and given out all the Friendship Bracelets to our friends."

"Not all of them," Dora smiled as she looked in Swiper's bag. There was one bracelet left.

Dora took the last Friendship Bracelet from the bag and gave it to Swiper.

"This one is for Swiper," said Dora. "Because he helped return the Friendship Bracelets to all our friends around the world."

"Oh, mannn!" exclaimed Swiper happily.

Dora and Swiper took Jessica, Marlie, Kathleen and Charlie back home to Brooklin, and it was time to say goodbye.

"Thank you for helping us deliver the Friendship Bracelets to our friends around the world!" said Dora to Jessica, Marlie, Kathleen and Charlie. "¡Gracias!"

"Thank you!" replied Jessica. "It was a great adventure!"

"And remember, every time you wear your Friendship Bracelet, think of me and all our friends around the world," said Dora.

"Happy Friendship Day!"

Dora's Sleepover

¡Hola! I am Dora. I am having a sleepover with my best friend, Boots, at his tree house.

"Jessica, why don't you join us?" asked Dora.

"I'd love to!" replied Jessica. "Can Marlie, Kathleen and Charlie come too?"

"Of course! We'll all go," said Dora. "Mami has made some cookies for us to take." Dora packed Backpack with her pajamas, flashlight, sleeping bag, and book of pirate stories.

Map showed them the best way to get to Boots'
tree house.

On the way, they spotted someone
behind a tree. It was Swiper.
He wanted to swipe the cookies.

"Oh no! Everybody say, Swiper,
no swiping!" called Dora.

We stopped Swiper!

"Oh, look! There's Boots' tree house," said Dora. "¡Hola! Boots! Jessica, Marlie, Kathleen and Charlie are joining us for our sleepover!"

They climbed the ladder to get to Boots' tree house.

"Welcome everyone! Now all our friends are here, it's time for our sleepover!" Boots said excitedly.

Soon, the sun started to go down and Dora, Jessica, Marlie, Kathleen, Charlie, and Boots put on their pajamas.

They laid out their sleeping bags and settled in for the night.

Dora offered them all cookies that her Mami had made especially for their sleepover. Yum! They were hungry!

Dora had a surprise for Boots, too. She handed him her pirate story book.

"Yeah!" exclaimed Boots.
"I love pirates!"

"We'll take turns reading to you, Boots," said Jessica. "Then we can make up our own pirate stories."

Soon, it was dark and the moon shone brightly through the window. The friends were getting tired and it was time to go to sleep.

"Thank you for sharing your sleepover with us," said Jessica. "We've had so much fun! Good night, Dora. Good night, Boots. Good night, everybody."

"I'm glad you could all join us. Good night everybody!" replied Dora. "Sleep tight!"

Boots yawned and snuggled into his sleeping bag.

Soon they were all sleeping peacefully.

For our entire selection of books, please visit www.identitydirect.ca

This personalized Dora the Explorer book was especially created for Jessica Mahoney of Brooklin with love from Nana & Papa.

Additional books ordered may be mailed separately — please allow a few days for differences in delivery times.

If you would like to receive additional My Adventure Book forms, please contact:

My Adventure Books

PO Box 6000
Brampton ON L6V 4N3
Phone: 905 840 4141
www.identitydirect.ca

0375 004370 0001 01 DS)280

0 3 7 5 0 0 4 3 7 0 0 0 0 1 0 1